THE WIND IN THE WILLOWS

by KENNETH GRAHAME

#6 Restless Rat

Adapted by Laura Driscoll

Illustrated by Ann Iosa

STERLING

New York / London

www.sterlingpublishing.com/kids

STERLING and the distinctive Sterling logo are registered trademarks
of Sterling Publishing Co., Inc.

Library of Congress Cataloging-in-Publication Data Available

Lot #: 02/10
10 9 8 7 6 5 4 3 2 1

Published by Sterling Publishing Co., Inc.
387 Park Avenue South, New York, NY 10016
© 2010 by Sterling Publishing Co., Inc.
Illustrations © 2010 by Ann Iosa
Distributed in Canada by Sterling Publishing
c/o Canadian Manda Group, 165 Dufferin Street
Toronto, Ontario, Canada M6K 3H6
Distributed in the United Kingdom by GMC Distribution Services
Castle Place, 166 High Street, Lewes, East Sussex, England BN7 1XU
Distributed in Australia by Capricorn Link (Australia) Pty. Ltd.
P.O. Box 704, Windsor, NSW 2756, Australia

Printed in China

Sterling ISBN 978 1-4027-6730-2

For information about custom editions, special sales, premium
and corporate purchases, please contact Sterling Special Sales
Department at 800-805-5489 or specialsales@sterlingpublishing.com.

Contents

Changes

Rat loved summer at the river.

The air was warm.

The trees were leafy and green.

But today Rat felt restless.

There was something new in the air.

So Rat took a walk
away from the river.
He walked across a field.

Soon he met some field mice.

"Hello, Ratty!" said a mouse.

"Want to lend a hand?"

The mice were busy.

They were packing food.

They were getting ready to move

to their winter homes.

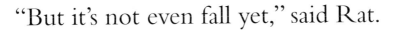

"But it's not even fall yet," said Rat.

"We know," said the mouse.

"But we want to get an early start!"

Rat headed back to the river.
There he saw some birds.
They were talking about
their flight south for the winter.

"Already?" asked Rat.

One bird told Rat,

"We are not leaving yet.

We are just making plans."

Rat did not like this.

Soon the birds would leave.

Soon the mice would leave.

Rat would be left behind.

Rat walked some more.

He sat down by a dusty road.

Then Rat heard a sound.

Rat heard footsteps!

Someone was coming down the road.

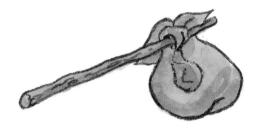

The Sea Rat

It was another rat—
a traveling rat.
He carried his things
in a blue handkerchief.
He was dusty from the road.
He looked very tired.
Without a word,
the traveler sat down by Rat.

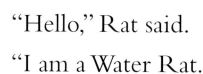

"Hello," Rat said.

"I am a Water Rat.

Who are you?"

"I am a Sea Rat," he said,

"and I am headed back to the sea."

That sounded exciting to Rat.

Then he realized it was lunchtime.

He knew the Sea Rat must be hungry.

"My house is close by," said Rat.
"Would you like to come
and have some lunch?"

"Why, thank you!" said the Sea Rat.
"But . . . could we eat out here?"

A picnic! thought Rat.
What a great idea!
So Rat hurried home
to get some food.

Lunch

At home, Rat got out a picnic basket.
He packed bread and cheese
and sausage and grapes.
Then he hurried back to the Sea Rat.
Together, they unpacked the lunch.

"Wonderful!" said the hungry Sea Rat
when he saw the food.
The Sea Rat said nothing else for a while.
He was too busy eating.

Soon, however,
the Sea Rat began to talk.

He told Rat about ships.

He told Rat about the sea.

He told Rat about kings and queens

and cities and towns

and all the places he had been.

Rat got to thinking:

I want to be a Sea Rat, too!

Soon the Sea Rat stood up.

"I have to go now," he said.

"But you should come, too!

Have an adventure with me!"

He started walking down the road.

Then he turned and looked back at Rat.

"Catch up with me if you like!"

Rat watched the Sea Rat go.

He watched him until

he couldn't see him anymore.

Then Rat got up.

He walked home.

He started to pack!

Good-bye, Rat?

Rat packed a bag.

He picked out a walking stick.

Then he opened the door to leave.

And guess who was there, about
to come in? Mole!

Mole was Rat's best friend.

"Where are you going?" asked Mole.

"Away!" said Rat.

"Like everyone else!"

Mole was worried.

Rat was leaving the river?

Rat *loved* the river.

Mole pulled Rat back inside.

He sat Rat down.

"What happened?" asked Mole.

So Rat told him about the mice,

the birds, and the Sea Rat.

Then Mole understood.
All day Rat had heard reasons
to leave the river.

Maybe now he just needed
some reasons to stay.
So Mole began to talk
about life on the river—
about the fall harvest,
about picking red apples
and watching the leaves change colors.
He talked about all the good reasons
why Rat should stay.

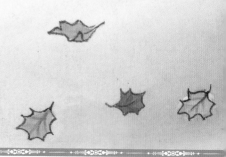

Rat listened.

His eyes got brighter.

His ears perked up.

He was remembering why
he loved his home.

Then he remembered
one more great thing about home.

Mole was there!

Then it was clear to Rat—
there was nowhere he would rather
be than home sweet home.